NICKELODEON

SpongeBob SquarePants

The Great Escape

adapted by Emily Sollinger
based on the teleplay by Paul Tibbitt, Steven Banks,
Luke Brookshier, and Nate Cash
illustrated by The Artifact Group

W9-BFZ-711

SCHOLASTIC INC.
New York Toronto London Auckland Sydney
Mexico City New Delhi Hong Kong Buenos Aires

Stephen Hillenburg

Based on the TV series *SpongeBob SquarePants*® created by Stephen Hillenburg as seen on Nickelodeon®

ISBN-13: 978-0-545-19754-0
ISBN-10: 0-545-19754-6

12 11 10 9 8 7 6 5 4 3 2 1   9 10 11 12 13 14/0

Printed in the U.S.A.

First Scholastic printing, October 2009

Bllllaaare! Bllllaaare! SpongeBob's alarm woke him suddenly from his sweet dreams.

"Oh boy, Gary! It's the day I've been waiting for!" shouted SpongeBob. "Today is the single greatest day of my career. It's the eleventy-seventh anniversary of the Krusty Krab. I cannot be late!" he continued, as he rushed around his house getting ready.

When SpongeBob arrived at the Krusty Krab, there was a line of customers snaking out from the door for miles. He bounced along on top of their heads.

"I'm sorry, everyone," said SpongeBob as he stepped on heads left and right, "but Mr. Krabs needs me." SpongeBob wiggled his way through the nearly closed front door and landed right in the arms of a waiting Mr. Krabs.

"Today is a big day for the Krusty Krab," Mr. Krabs reminded SpongeBob and Squidward. "I'm sure Plankton is going to try to steal my secret Krabby Patty recipe."

Then Mr. Krabs showed them a map of secret underground tunnels connected to the Krusty Krab. "Study this map, stay extra vigilant, and don't fall asleep on the job, Squidward! I even brought in some extra security," he announced as Patrick appeared proudly.

"Aye, aye, Mr. Krabs!" said SpongeBob excitedly.

Meanwhile, over at Plankton's restaurant, the always-empty Chum Bucket . . .

"A thousand and three times I've almost had that recipe, and a thousand and three times I've failed!" cried Plankton to Karen, his computer wife. "I give up! Krabs has won!"

He thought back on all of the times Mr. Krabs launched him out into the sky for trying to steal the secret recipe.

"But today is the perfect day to steal the recipe!" encouraged Karen. "Krabs will be so distracted by all of the festivities. You can do it!"

Back at the Krusty Krab, Mr. Krabs gave SpongeBob a very important job—doing the decorations for the eleventy-seventh celebration. SpongeBob was thrilled.

"Go ahead and decorate it any way you want," said Mr. Krabs, handing SpongeBob fifty cents.

"Wow, fifty cents! Mr. Krabs, are you sure? That's double the eleventy-sixth anniversary decorations' budget! Woo-hoo!"

SpongeBob was proud to show off his decorating skills, and even prouder to show Mr. Krabs his special creation.

"I now present to you my ode to the Krabby Patty!" said SpongeBob, leading the group into the freezer and showing off a larger-than-life Krabby Patty sculpture. "It's made entirely out of ice!"

"Wow! It's *ice*-squisite!" exclaimed Patrick with a giggle.

"All right! Let's get this thing out of here. My customers are waiting," said Mr. Krabs.

But as they tried to push the heavy sculpture out into the restaurant, SpongeBob slipped and—*Boink!*—he bounced off the wall and knocked the freezer door shut!

"We're locked in!" cried SpongeBob after the door slammed loudly.

"There's only one way out of here," said Mr. Krabs. "Through the air ducts."

They tumbled through a maze of air ducts. After several wrong turns they finally barreled through a door.

"Oh, barnacles!" grumbled Mr. Krabs. "I thought this was the exit, but it's just my surveillance room." Television monitors all around the room revealed crowds of hungry customers getting bigger and louder.

"We want Krabby Patties! We want Krabby Patties!" they chanted.

SpongeBob and the crew went back into the air ducts to look for the exit. At that very moment Plankton squeezed through a vent from outside of the Krusty Krab and into the air ducts, smashing right into SpongeBob.

"Why must you always ruin my plans, SpongeBob?" Plankton complained.

"Aha! I'll bet you are trying to steal the Krabby Patty recipe again, aren't you?" asked SpongeBob.

"What? Uh . . . okay, fine. You caught me!" Plankton replied.

"All of this reminds me of the time Mr. Krabs first shared the Krabby Patty recipe with me," SpongeBob told Plankton. "But I don't want to bore you with my silly old stories."

"Oh, you couldn't possibly bore me!" Plankton said eagerly.

"Well, Mr. Krabs called me into his office . . . ," SpongeBob recalled dreamily.

"'SpongeBob, you've been working here awhile now so I think I can trust you,' said Mr. Krabs. 'It's time I told you the Krabby Patty formula! Follow me. We need to go where no one will ever hear us.'"

"And so we climbed the rockiest mountains, hiked through the deepest jungles, and sailed the saltiest seas until we finally found the safest place in the whole world."

"Then Mr. Krabs leaned in close. He told me I could never share what he was about to tell me with another living soul!"

Plankton took out a pen and paper, ready to scribble down the recipe at any minute!

"Plankton!" yelled Mr. Krabs, creeping up from behind. "Taking advantage of all this reminiscing, I see. You'll never get my recipe. Not even in a flashback!" Mr. Krabs picked up Plankton between his fingertips and launched him yet again into the air ducts.

"We want Krabby Patties! We want Krabby Patties!" The hungry customers were getting louder.

"We've got to get out of here now!" shouted Mr. Krabs. "These people want to spend money in my restaurant!"

Everyone sighed. They were so frustrated and sick of being stuck in the air ducts!

"SpongeBob, if you'd never come to Bikini Bottom in the first place, none of this would be happening!" complained Squidward.

SpongeBob remembered when he first arrived in Bikini Bottom. He searched far and wide for the perfect house and finally found it—home, sweet pineapple! "Oh, Squidward," said SpongeBob. "Aren't you glad I moved in that day?" he asked. "If I hadn't, we wouldn't be neighbors, and I never would have met Patrick, and . . ."

"What's that?" interrupted Mr. Krabs as he spotted a crumpled piece of paper on the ground. "Why, it's an old Krabby Patty wrapper. This takes me back to the old days," he recalled. "Back then Krabby Patties only cost ten cents! I can't believe how much money I was missing out on by charging so little!"

"Those were the good old days," said SpongeBob, remembering his very first visit to the Krusty Krab. "Oh, I can't believe we are missing the eleventy-seventh anniversary celebration! We've got to get out there."

"We'll never get out of here," grumbled Squidward. Mr. Krabs and Patrick sighed in agreement. They were ready to give up.

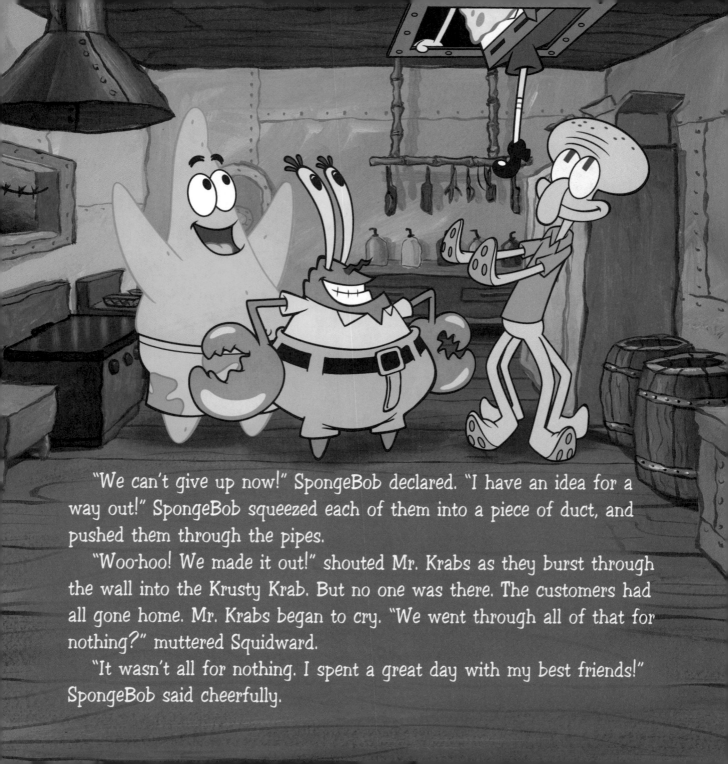

"We can't give up now!" SpongeBob declared. "I have an idea for a way out!" SpongeBob squeezed each of them into a piece of duct, and pushed them through the pipes.

"Woo-hoo! We made it out!" shouted Mr. Krabs as they burst through the wall into the Krusty Krab. But no one was there. The customers had all gone home. Mr. Krabs began to cry. "We went through all of that for nothing?" muttered Squidward.

"It wasn't all for nothing. I spent a great day with my best friends!" SpongeBob said cheerfully.

Then SpongeBob began to sing a song all about how much he loved the Krusty Krab. His tune echoed throughout all of Bikini Bottom. One by one, the hungry customers stopped what they were doing and followed the music all the way back to the Krusty Krab.

"Come on, people! Let's go get some Krabby Patties!" SpongeBob cheered to the crowd.

Meanwhile Plankton dusted himself off after flying through the air ducts and out a vent.

"I'm a failure!" Plankton cried. But it was Plankton's lucky day—he had landed right beside the bottle containing the secret Krabby Patty recipe! Quickly he picked up the bottle and carried it toward the front door.

At the very same moment a horde of customers led by SpongeBob came bounding through the door, trampling Plankton, and knocking the recipe out of his grasp.

"Did somebody order a Krabby Pa—*Whoa!*" called SpongeBob as he slipped on the bottle holding the recipe. The bottle rolled over to Mr. Krabs.

"What's my secret recipe doing here?" gasped Mr. Krabs as he took a closer look. "Oh, Plankton, I should have known!" he said angrily. He peeled Plankton off the bottle and launched him once and for all out of the Krusty Krab!

"What a day!" exclaimed SpongeBob. "Happy eleventy-seventh anniversary, Krusty Krab!" he said as he flipped a patty.